Winter Is the Warmest Season

Lauren Stringer

Harcourt, Inc.

Orlando   Austin   New York   San Diego   Toronto   London

Special thanks to Cooper for sharing his wise winter thoughts

www.HarcourtBooks.com

Library of Congress Cataloging-in-Publication Data
Stringer, Lauren.
Winter is the warmest season/by Lauren Stringer.
p.   cm.
Summary: A child describes pleasant ways to stay warm during the winter, from sipping
hot chocolate and eating grilled cheese sandwiches to wearing woolly sweaters and sitting
near a glowing fireplace.
[1. Winter—Fiction.   2. Seasons—Fiction]   I. Title.
PZ7.S9183Win   2006
[E]—dc22   2005005723
ISBN-13: 978-0-15-204967-6   ISBN-10: 0-15-204967-3

H G F

Manufactured in China

The illustrations in this book were done in Lascaux acrylics on Fabriano 140 lb. watercolor paper.
The display lettering was created by Judythe Sieck.
The text type was set in Dante.
Color separations by Bright Arts Ltd., Hong Kong
Manufactured by South China Printing Company, Ltd., China
This book was printed on totally chlorine-free Stora Enso Matte paper.
Production supervision by Pascha Gerlinger
Designed by Lauren Stringer and Lydia D'moch

For my dear Inkslingers,
and for Matthew, Ruby, and Cooper

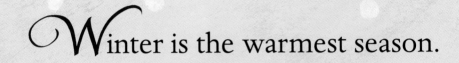

Winter is the warmest season.

Most people think it's summer,
with its long steamy days.
But not me.

My world is warmest in winter.

When winter comes, my jacket
puffs warm with feathers,

my hat grows earflaps,

my pants hide deep
in fuzzy boots,

and my hands wear
warm woolly sweaters.

When winter comes, summer's plants and animals sleep deep under thick blankets of snow,

while the snowmen I build dance on top,
wearing warm wraparound scarves.

When winter comes, my iced summer's milk turns to hot chocolate. Cold jelly sandwiches turn into grilled cheeses.

Hot soups, hot pies,
and oven-hot breads
make winter the warmest
for the inside of me.

When winter comes,
summer's cool fans hide
in dark basements . . .

while sleeping radiators awake
to their dragon selves, banging
and hissing and pouring heat
all through my house.

When winter comes,
cats sit on laps
instead of windowsills.

Even nights are warmer in winter.

Fires burn in fireplaces.
Candles burn in candleplaces.

I think parties
are warmer in winter.

And when summer's cool swims

turn into winter's hot baths . . .

I know my pajamas
will grow big warm feet.

My bed is warmest in winter,
piled high with blankets of plaid,
blankets striped yellow,
and a blue, starry quilt on top.

In winter, bodies sit closer,
books last longer, and
hugs squeeze the warmest.

Even friends are warmer.

And in winter, when it's the very warmest
and I close my sleepy eyes,
I might dream of summer . . .

just to cool me off!

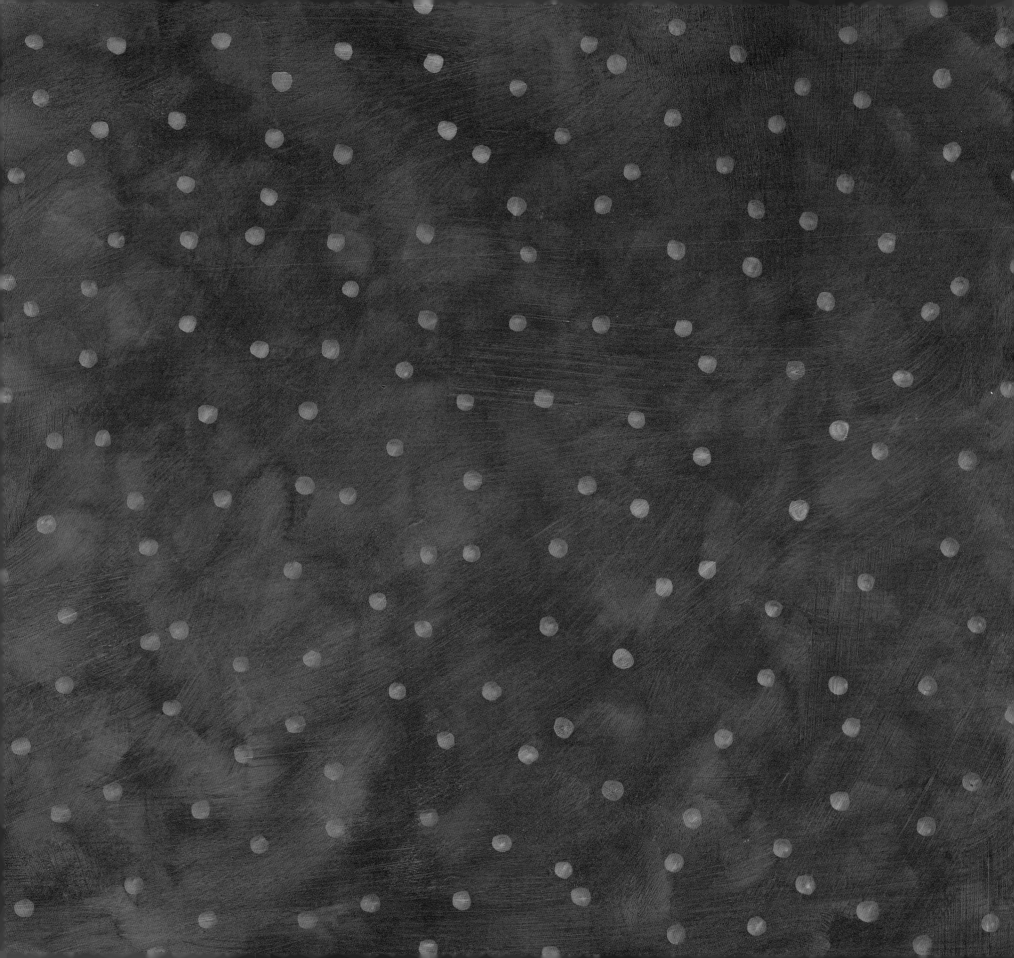